Short "u" and Long "u"
Play a Game

Library of Congress Cataloging-in-Publication Data
Moncure, Jane Belk.
Short "u" and long "u" play a game / by Jane Belk Moncure ; illustrated by Norman Young.
p. cm.
Summary: Short u and Long u introduce the long and short "u" sounds.
ISBN 1-56766-932-8 (library bound)
[1. English language—Vowels—Fiction.]   I. Young, N. (Norman), ill. II. Title.
PZ7.M739 Sj 2001
[E]—dc21
00-010852

Short "u" and Long "u"
Play a Game

Jane Belk Moncure
illustrated by Norman Young

This is  . He has a special sound.

Umbrella

begins with his short "u" sound.

So does up ↑.

Open up the umbrella!

This is  . She has a different sound.

Unicorn

begins with her long "u" sound.

So does ukulele.

Can you hear the  short u

and the long u sounds?

up↑

umbrella

short
u

One day, Short "u" said,
"Let's play a game. I will look
for my sound in words.

ukulele

unicorn

You can look for your sound
in words. We'll see who can
find the most words."

Short u found underclothes,

lots of underclothes...

on a clothesline.

"I will win!" he said.

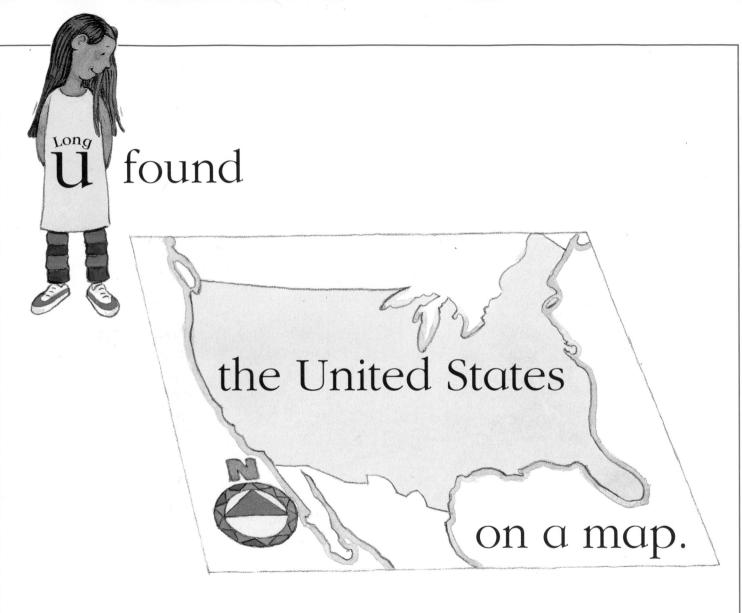

Long **u** found

the United States

on a map.

She also found...

uniforms, lots of uniforms.

"I will win!" she said.

unicorn

uniforms

United States

ukulele

counted. "I win," she said.
"I have the most words."

umbrella

up ↑

underclothes

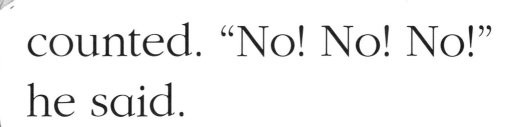

counted. "No! No! No!" he said.

"I will use my eyes

and 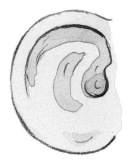 ears.

My sound hides in words.
I will find words with my
sound in the middle of them."

Short **u** found

a duck

in a mud puddle.

Then  found a dump truck

stuck in the mud!

He also found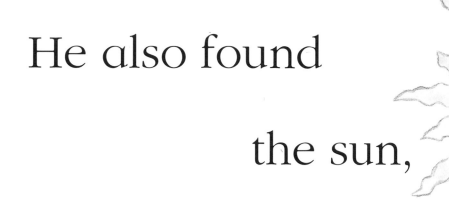

the sun,

buttercups,

a butterfly...

and pups,

pups,

pups!

"Now I win," said short **u** .

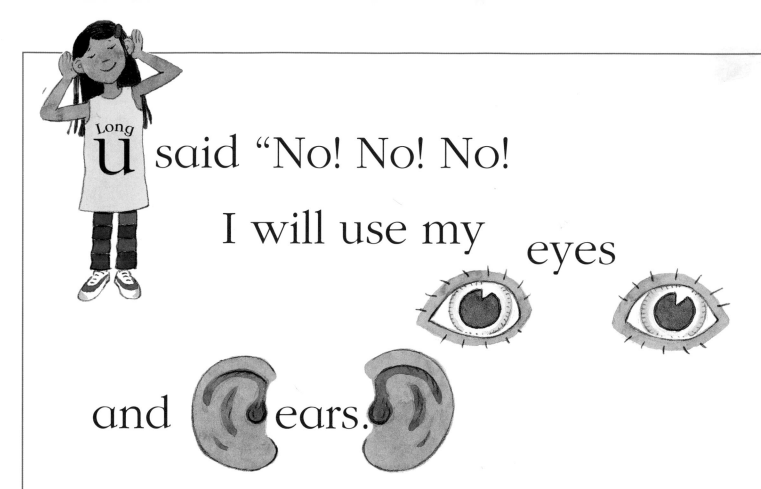

Long **u** said "No! No! No!

I will use my eyes

and ears.

My sound hides in words, too.
I will find words with my
sound in the middle of them."

She found two mules,

a cucumber,

and a cupid.

"Now I win!" said _{long} **u** .

up↑

underclothes

umbrella

dump truck

sun

butterfly

short u

duck

pups

mud puddle

Can you tell who won?

cupid

cucumber

ukulele

mule

United States

unicorn

long
u

Can you read more words with  short u?

bus

puppet

gum

bunny

brush

skunk

bubbles

bucket

Can you read more words with 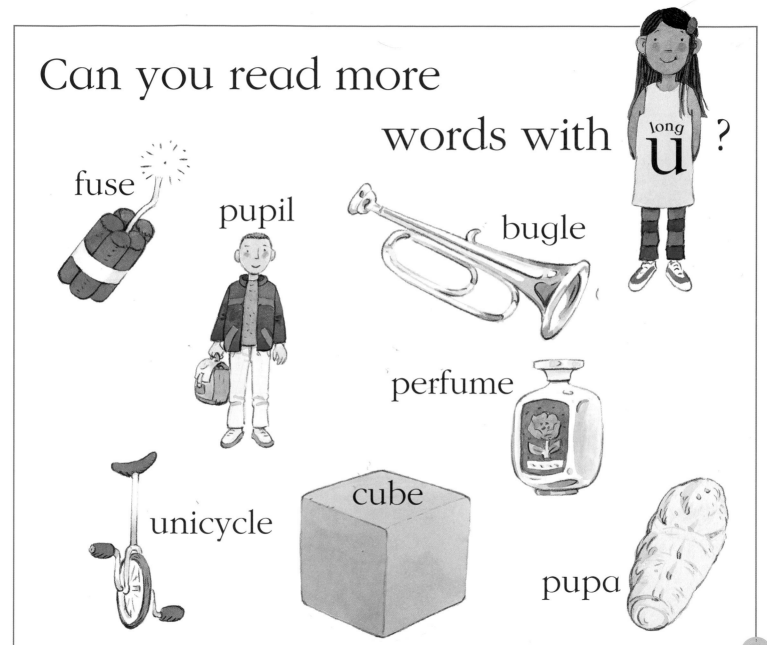 long u ?

fuse

pupil

bugle

perfume

unicycle

cube

pupa

Now you make up a game!

ABOUT THE AUTHOR AND ILLUSTRATOR

Jane Belk Moncure began her writing career when she was in kindergarten. She has never stopped writing. Many of her children's stories and poems have been published, to the delight of young readers, including her son Jim, whose childhood experiences found their way into many of her books.

Mrs. Moncure's writing is based upon an active career in early childhood education. A recipient of an M.A. degree from Columbia University, Mrs. Moncure has taught and directed nursery, kindergarten, and primary grade programs in California, New York, Virginia, and North Carolina. As a former member of the faculties of Virginia Commonwealth University and the University of Richmond, she taught prospective teachers in early childhood education.

Mrs. Moncure has travelled extensively abroad, studying early childhood programs in the United Kingdom, The Netherlands, and Switzerland. She was the first president of the Virginia Association for Early Childhood Education and received its award for outstanding service to young children. A resident of North Carolina, Mrs. Moncure is currently a full-time writer and educational consultant. She is married to Dr. James A. Moncure, former vice president of Elon College.

Norman Young spent his childhood on a small farm nestled at the foot of the Preseli Hills in Pembrokeshire, South West Wales. He started his artistic career as a film animator in London and then in Zagreb. Eventually he settled in Devon, where he lives beside a river that runs between the moors and the sea. It was here that he started his work as an illustrator of children's books. Norman has always had a lifelong interest in history and travel. Taking a month off work each year, he visits new places either by train or by bicycle—and he never goes anywhere without his sketchbook.